This book belongs to

....

Also by Matt Beighton

Poetry

Tig You're It: And other poems from the playground

The Shadowland Chronicles

The Spyglass and the Cherry Tree

The Shadowed Eye

Monstacademy Series

The Halloween Parade

The Egyptian Treasure

The Grand High Monster

The Machu Picchu Mystery

The Magic Knight

For Younger Readers

Spot The Dot

For Phoebe and Willow

MONSTACADEMY
THE MAGIC KNIGHT
A CHOOSE YOUR OWN MONSTACADEMY STORY

Copyright © Matt Beighton 2018

Matt Beighton has asserted his right under the Copyright, Designs and Patents Act, 1988, to be identified as the author of this work.

All rights reserved. This book or any portion thereof may not be reproduced, lent, hired, circulated or used in any manner whatsoever without the express written permission of the author.

Printed in the United Kingdom

First Printing, 2018

A CIP catalogue record for this book is available from the British Library.

ISBN (Standard Edition): 978-1-9997244-5-0
ISBN (Dyslexia Friendly): 978-1-9997244-9-8

www.mattbeighton.co.uk
www.monstacademy.com

The Magic Knight

Welcome

Hello and welcome to The Magic Knight, an interactive adventure set at the fictional school of Monstacademy. You may find it easier and recognise more of the characters if you have read the other books in the series starting with The Halloween Parade but, in case you haven't, I will give you a quick rundown here.

Monroe's Academy for the Different, or Monstacademy as it is known amongst the children who attend, is a school for monsters. There are vampires, werewolves, witches and wizards and plenty more besides. One of the characters that you will meet in this book, Trixie Grimble, isn't a monster at all. She was sent to Monstacademy in The Halloween Parade after her own, ordinary school closed down.

Now, a little information on how this book works. It doesn't work like an ordinary book with chapters that follow on from each other. Instead, it is broken up into smaller sections that aren't in order at all. This makes it much more exciting as you don't know what is coming next.

The only thing that is the same as normal is that you **start at number 1**.

Throughout the book you will be able to control what your character does and how the story progresses. Some of these decisions will be made by you and some will be taken out of your hands. You will need a normal, six-sided dice to help make some of the decisions.

Along the way you will be asked to perform actions. These will be **in bold writing**. You may be asked to add things to your backpack; these should be written down on the adventure sheet.

You can download blank copies of the adventure sheet from **www.mattbeighton.co.uk/media**.

In all, there are nearly twenty different endings to this book! However, only three of them are good and mean that you successfully complete the adventure! If you do complete the adventure, I recommend you go back and take a different course to see if you can complete all three exciting endings. The rest? Well, let's just say they aren't quite as happy an ending for your character!

Oh, whilst I remember, there are five gold coins hidden in various scenes throughout the book. See if you can find them all!

Happy adventuring!

Matt Beighton

You will need:

A copy of the adventure sheet

A pen or pencil

A regular, six-sided dice

A sense of adventure!

My Adventure Sheet

My species
☐ Werewolf   ☐ Vampire   ☐ Witch/Wizard

My backpack

My notes

My collected coins

The Magic Knight

1

You look at the letter that the postman has just slipped through your letter box one more time. You read it again to make sure you aren't imagining things.

Dear sir or madam,

Further to your recent application, we are delighted to offer you a place at Monroe's Academy for the Different for the coming academic year.

You can't believe that you got in, after months of worrying it is finally happening. You are going to Monstacademy!

The letter has a form attached for all of your personal information. You eagerly fill it all in until there is only one box left.

The Magic Knight

Please indicate what type of monster you are.

Roll a dice.

If you roll a 1 or 2 go to **91**

If you roll a 3 or 4 go to **13**

If you roll a 5 or 6 go to **103**

<u>2</u>

You start to sweat when the lock just won't budge. Heston looks at you with disappointment and hands the picks over to Dilbert who opens it easily.

Heston pushes the door open to reveal a dark room and pushes you through first. You hear the door slam shut behind you and the lock click.

Your new friends laugh at you

The Magic Knight

through the door and Heston tells you he's off to find a teacher.

You slide down the door realising that you've been trapped. No doubt a detention will follow but, for now, you're stuck where you are.

It looks like you definitely made the wrong choice following Heston. Your first day at Monstacademy has ended in complete disaster! Bad luck! Game over!

3

You can't resist any longer and reach up to scratch your itchy ear. Unfortunately, moving your arms means that Gloria loses her grip on your collar and your stomach lurches as you hang momentarily in thin air before starting to plummet towards

The Magic Knight

the rocky ground below.

   Just as you start to see your life flashing in front of your eyes, the wind is knocked out of you by a thick branch growing out of the tower wall. You cling on for dear life and close your eyes until you get your breath back and you stop seeing stars.

   When you open your eyes you see a shiny gold coin wedged in the crack between two old stones. You reach out and grab it. **Congratulations, you found one of the gold coins!**

   Next to the coin is a horrible, scraggly weed growing out from between the old stones. It looks very familiar but it takes you a minute to remember that it is Swine's Armpit. You remember that Mr Snickletinkle says that it will help you to levitate

The Magic Knight

when you are desperate and you realise that this could help you float down to the ground.

You tear off a handful of leaves and try desperately to remember what it was that the teacher said to do with them.

To chew the leaves, go to **118**

To suck the leaves, go to **38**

To swallow the leaves, go to **17**

<u>4</u>

You push open the door and step into the darkness. Specks of dust float through the air and look like stars in the streams of light from the windows high in the ceiling.

Behind you, the door clicks shut and you hear Heston and his friends

The Magic Knight

giggling to themselves.

Your investigation into the mystery of the Magic Knight has come to an unhappy conclusion. Bad luck! Game over!

5

As you try to get your breath back you can hear Heston arguing with Miss Brimstone on the other side of the door. She is berating him for wasting her time but he is adamant that he saw you all trying to break in to the headmistress's office.

Roll a dice.

If you roll a 1, 2 or 3, go to **115**

If you roll a 4, 5 or 6, go to **28**

The Magic Knight

6

You remember the key in your backpack and pull it out looking sheepish. You explain to your friends where you go it from and decide to try it out on Miss Flopsbottom's door. You put the key to the lock and watch as it flickers and morphs through several different shapes until it settles on a long silver key with a heart shaped head. You slide it into the lock and it clicks open without even turning the key.

Go to **80**

7

You arrive at your science lesson in time for you all to take a seat together around a cauldron. Mr Snickletinkle, the science teacher, explains that today's lesson is all

The Magic Knight

about levitation potions.

"In a pinch," the old vampire drones, "you may suck the leaf of a small weed called a Swine's Armpit." The teacher points to a picture on the wall of a horrible, scraggly looking weed. "You may find that this allows you to float a few inches above the floor but it will never be enough to let you float amongst the clouds! For that, you need this potion!"

Mr Snickletinkle explains how to mix the potion whilst you and Colin try to flick pebbles into the cauldron. Gloria and Trixie look at you angrily but don't say anything.

Eventually the teacher stops droning on and Trixie and Gloria rush off to pick out the ingredients for the potion. When they return, you and

The Magic Knight

Colin start to measure them out.

A pinch of bumblebee eyelashes

A smidge of frog's tears

A dozen lizard toenails

Half an owl's hoot (it doesn't specify whether it should be the Twit or the Twoo)

And finally, some *troll's bogeys*.

Unfortunately, the number of troll's bogeys is smudged and covered in grease. Colin thinks it looks like a 3 but it could also be a 2 or an 8. It's up to you to decide how many bogeys to add to the potion.

To add 2 troll's bogeys, go to **44**

To add 3 troll's bogeys, go to **68**

To add 8 troll's bogeys, go to **47**

The Magic Knight

8

You follow Gloria as she leads the way back out of the caves and into the stream. You don't waste any time racing back up to the castle and straight up the steps to Miss Brimstone's office where the Magic Knight is just leaving. He nods and thanks you for your help before heading back down the steps. You notice that he is wearing a sunhat and carrying a stuffed suitcase.

Miss Flopsbottom pokes her head around the door and invites you all in. You take a seat again on the hard, wooden bench and wait to see what the two teachers have to say.

The headmistress says: "Gloria, Colin, Trixie and our new friend, you have saved Monstacademy from a

The Magic Knight

terrible fate. And not for the first time!" This was to the other three, but you feel proud to have achieved something so important. "There is nothing that I can offer you to make up for what you have done but I would like to give you a little something to show my gratitude." Miss Flopsbottom leans forward and hangs a gold medal around your neck. It shines in the sunlight streaming in through the window.

You may not have been at Monstacademy for long, but you know that you are going to like it here!

Congratulations, you've solved the mystery of the Magic Knight!

9

As you turn to leave, Heston notices what you are doing and throws a

The Magic Knight

bottle of potion over your head before you can react. You feel every inch of your body freeze solid, although you aren't cold at all. You realise that the only things that you can move are your eyeballs and you frantically look around as Heston and Kevin burst out laughing.

They pack up their bottles and blow out the torches. You hear the door lock and realise that you are stuck in the storeroom alone until you defrost in a day's time. Meanwhile, Heston will be able to take control of the whole school. **It looks like your first day at Monstacademy has ended in disaster! Bad luck! Game over!**

10

You follow the passage to right and

The Magic Knight

stagger forwards. The roof starts to get lower and lower and you hunch over. Without warning the floor gives way and you drop into a sludge-filled pit. You sink up to your knees and cry out for help.

After a while you hear Gloria shouting down out of the darkness. She tells you that Colin and Trixie have gone for help but for now you are stuck down here in the hole. **It looks like you won't be solving the mystery of the Magic Knight today! Bad luck! Game over!**

11

The lock spins and the door creaks open to reveal a dark room beyond. Heston pats you on the back and congratulates you on doing a brilliant job for him. He gives you a gold coin as a reward. "You're one of us now!" he says. **Congratulations, you found one of the gold coins!**

Go to **124**

<u>12</u>

Just in time, the lock clicks open and you all fall into the room and slam the door behind you. You grab a set of keys from Miss Flopsbottom's desk and use them to lock the door.

Go to **5**

<u>13</u>

You are a werewolf! Most of the time you are pretty normal, even if you are a bit hairy! You are very good at knowing what type of moon it will be and have a good sense of the weather. If it's a clear night and a full moon, you turn into a small, dribbling

The Magic Knight

wolf!

Don't worry though, you've learnt how to control yourself when you are a wolf and the only thing you're likely to do to embarrass yourself now is have a wee up against a lamppost. Still, it's probably something to avoid if you can!

Good luck with your first day at Monstacademy.

Go to **56**

14

After you've spent nearly an hour trying to pick the lock with one of Gloria's hairgrips, your friend sighs heavily and with a poof turns into a bat. You all watch as she flutters out of the window and disappears.

The Magic Knight

After a minute you hear a rattling on the other side of the door and it swings open to reveal a grinning Gloria holding a set of keys.

You all enter and lock the door behind you.

Go to **80**

15

You decide that the key might be valuable in your quest. **Add the Master Key to your backpack.** You decide to tell your friends about it as soon as they return from the Dark Section.

Go to **50**

16

You lean in for a closer look at the glass door and realise that there is

The Magic Knight

something strange about the lock. It hasn't been picked from the outside and it doesn't appear to be broken but there are scuffs and scratches on the inside, as though something *inside* the cabinet has tried to pick it open in the past.

Gloria wanders over and you explain to her what you have found and that it doesn't make any sense. Why would the Magic Knight pick his own lock from the inside? The vampire starts to smile a curious little smile but before she can explain why the bell rings to signal the start of your next lesson.

You all rush off to the science lab. Go to **7**

17

You push the handful of leaves into

The Magic Knight

your mouth and swallow hard. Luckily they don't taste of anything and you can soon feel them sliding down into your stomach. For a minute, nothing happens. Then, suddenly, you start to feel a lot lighter. It seems like the leaves are working until you realise that it's only your feet that feel lighter and, with a sickening jolt, they fly upwards and float above your head leaving you hanging upside down two hundred feet in the air.

Apparently swallowing the leaves has confused your body and it now thinks that up is down and down is up and your feet are trying their hardest to get back down to solid sky.

You scream out loud and Gloria flutters off to get help. You just hope it arrives before you leave the Earth's atmosphere and float off into space.

The Magic Knight

For now, your adventure is over! Bad luck! Game over!

18

Just as the ball of magic flies towards you, Miss Brimstone, the deputy-headmistress, pushes you out of the way and deflects it back towards the three witches. With a puff of smoke, they are all turned instantly into croaking frogs.

"I will deal with them later." Miss Brimstone says. "For now, you need to get off to your history lesson. Here is a map to help you, please try not to go wandering the corridors next time, I might not be here to save you!"

You take the map from Miss Brimstone and head straight to your lesson.

The Magic Knight

Add the Map of the School to your backpack.

Go to **84**

19

You get dressed for bed and wander over to your basket in the corner. You swipe the dog toys onto the floor and walk in a circle until you have it just the way you like it. You curl up into a ball and try to chew on your leg.

Eventually you fall asleep worrying about who might possibly want the magical suit of armour and what they plan to do with it.

Go to **126**

20

You sit down at a table in the hall and turn to your new friends. "What

The Magic Knight

is the suit of armour that's gone missing?" You ask. "Is it important?"

"I've never heard of it, it can't be!" Colin boasts.

Gloria rolls her eyes, "What you don't know, Colin Curlyton, would fill a very thick book! I heard a legend of a magical suit of armour, more of a magic knight really, that would protect its master from anyone who attacked his castle. I think it was a fairy-tale that my mother told me when I was a child. I can't remember much more than that now." She looks disappointed in herself for not remembering every little detail. "I do know one thing though, I bet we can guess who's behind this!"

At the front of the hall, Miss Flopsbottom starts to speak again.

The Magic Knight

To continue your conversation, go to **25**

To be quiet, go to **119**

<u>21</u>

You close your eyes and, with a loud pop, turn into a small wolf and hop up onto the windowsill where you see a small brown poodle looking back at you. Colin has clearly had the same idea!

As you perch on the sill you listen as Miss Brimstone and Heston enter the room and stand by the door. You look up and see Gloria hanging from the light fitting.

Heston is trying his hardest to look around the room but Miss Brimstone is holding him back. "The room is clearly empty young man.

The Magic Knight

I am beginning to suspect that you just wanted to snoop around the headmistress's office!" she grumbles as she escorts him out of the room and locks the door behind them.

You decide to have a quick look around the room before leaving.

Go to **28**

22

It doesn't take long to get to Miss Brimstone's office and as soon as you are through the door you sit down on the hard wooden bench against the wall.

"I've never seen anything like it!" she shouts. "Mr Snickletinkle might never be the same again!"

"I'm sorry Miss," says Gloria.

The Magic Knight

"We were distracted. We think we know what's happened to the Magic Knight."

Gloria explains to Miss Brimstone that she doesn't think the knight was stolen at all. She doesn't know what has happened to him yet, but she is sure that she can figure it out if Miss Brimstone just gives her a bit more time.

Miss Brimstone closes her eyes and pinches the bridge of her nose. **Roll your dice twice.**

If you roll two evens, go to **101**

Otherwise go to **37**

<u>23</u>

You hear Miss Brimstone enter the room and the hairs on the back of

The Magic Knight

your neck stand on end. You suddenly worry about your feet sticking out from underneath the curtain the curtain but it's too late to find another hiding place.

If you are a vampire, go to **57**

If you are a werewolf, go to **21**

Otherwise, go to **104**

24

The voices of your friends seem closer now although the echoes make it hard to tell for sure. You slow down to make sure you don't hit your head again. It doesn't take long before you find yourself at yet another branch in the path.

To follow the left passage, go to **79**

To head right, go to **10**

The Magic Knight

<u>25</u>

Miss Brimstone turns her head towards your whispered conversation and storms over to your table. She grabs you by the ears and drags you and your friends out into the corridor.

"Do you know how important the information that Miss Flopsbottom is about to tell you is?" She doesn't wait for you to answer before continuing, "Unless this suit of armour is found, this school is in grave peril. You would do well to close your mouths and open your ears!"

Roll a dice:

If you roll even, go to **69**

If you roll an odd number, go to **74**

The Magic Knight

26

You step through the doorway on the right and nearly trip down a flight of wooden steps hammered into the wall. The steps look old and rotten and there are a few missing in places. Leading off to the left is a set of newer, stone steps that climb higher into the mountain. You remember that you need to be climbing back up into the tower to find the old storeroom but you're not sure which set of steps to take.

To climb up steps go to **71**

To head downwards go to **46**

27

You head away from the hall and follow Heston Gobswaddle. He soon notices you tagging along and quickly

The Magic Knight

pulls you behind one of the big stone statues that line the hallway. He introduces you to his friends, Dilbert Trompton and Kevin Thimblenose and explains that he has something to show you all in a store room on the other side of school.

You try to remind him that you are supposed to be heading towards the main hall but he is confident that his dad will get him out of any trouble and that you can trust him. He promises that what he has to show you will be worth it.

To follow Heston, go to **127**

To make leave, go to **54**

28

In the distance you can hear Miss Brimstone shouting at Heston for

The Magic Knight

wasting her time when there are so many important things to be done around the school. You all laugh at his misfortune and breathe a sigh of relief before starting to have a good look around the office. Hopefully, Heston will be in detention for long enough to keep him out of your hair until you solve the mystery.

You continue looking around the office. Go to **80**

29

The room beyond the doorway is lit by an enormous chandelier that hangs from the ceiling. It is filled with spluttering candles. Underneath it, tied to a wooden post, is the Magic Knight. Somebody has tied a scarf around where the mouth should be.

"It doesn't work you know! He

The Magic Knight

thinks it will shut me up, but I don't have a mouth!" The knight's voice is deep and metallic with a little bit of an echo.

"Shut up! Just shut up and tell me how to control you!" Heston bursts out of the shadows starts hitting the Magic Knight around the head with his fists.

"Do you want me to shut up, or tell you? I can't do both!" You see a red light flicker on and off inside the knight's helmet, almost like a wink.

For the first time, Heston notices you all stood there watching and turns to face you. You can see tears streaking down his face and his cheeks are red.

"You thought you were so smart finding this place!" Heston shouts

The Magic Knight

at Gloria. "But you left the map out when you raced out of the library! I found it! I'm going to control the Magic Knight and then the world!" He looks crestfallen for a moment. "Except, well, the book on how to control him is in Latin and he won't read it for me! But now you are here, you will help me read it won't you?"

Gloria scoffs at the suggestion but you remember that you speak Latin.

To offer to help Heston go to **35**

To keep quiet go to **60**

30

Luckily, the balls bounces away behind the bookshelves and you hear the librarian mutter and moan and head off in that direction.

The Magic Knight

You rush over to the door to the Dark Section of the library and whisper as loudly as you dare for your friends to come back. They step out from behind the door startle you. Your heart beats so loudly that you are sure the librarian will hear it and come racing over.

Colin is carrying a large, leather-bound book called Monstrous and Magical Artifacts Vol. III. **Add Monstrous and Magical Artifacts Vol. III to your backpack.**

Trixie reminds you all that they know just the place to look at the book in private. She leads you down to the basement where she, Colin and Gloria put together their infamous Halloween Parade banner. Go to **70**

The Magic Knight

31

You pull **Monstrous and Magical Artifacts Vol. III** out of your backpack and open it to the page about the Magic Knight. You compare the footprints to the picture and realise that they are exactly the same.

To find out more you decide to head over to the museum to find out whatever you can about what has been happening to the knight more recently.

Go to **65**

32

You start to panic and feel the tingling sensation of magic in your fingertips. Just as you are about to burst with nervousness, a bright ball

The Magic Knight

of light flashes from your fingers and the lock clicks open. You dive through the door and slam it shut behind you. There is a set of keys on Miss Flopsbottom's desk and you use these to lock the door.

Go to **5**

33

You stagger through the door and are relieved to see that the passageway opens out and that the ground is much flatter underfoot. You stand up properly and are able to run for the first time since you entered the caves. Something shiny catches your eye as you walk past a pile of rocks. You wander over and find a gold coin. **Congratulations, you found one of the gold coins!**

You sprint as fast as you can until

The Magic Knight

the walls start to close in again and the ground becomes uneven. In your haste you haven't noticed that you have been running in a long spiral getting slowly lower with each turn.

By the time you realise, it is too late and you emerge back out into a very familiar passageway.

Go to **97**

34

You remember that you have a sketch of the footprints from Miss Flopsbottom's office and pull them out to compare with the picture in the book. You realise that the Magic Knight is the same suit of armour and that you are looking for the same thing.

It's obvious that you need to know

more about the recent history of the suit of armour and you all decide to head to the museum to speak to the curator. Go to **65**

35

You step forward and offer to help Heston translate the book. Gloria and the others look shocked but you have a plan. You ask Heston for the passage that you need to read to get the Magic Knight to obey you and he points to a small paragraph underneath a picture of the knight.

Quod dico hominem metallum aut rubigo in fundo Oceanum usque in sempiternum.

You take a deep breath and read aloud the words.

"Do what I say metal man or rust

The Magic Knight

forever at the bottom of the ocean."

The red lights shine brightly in the Magic Knight's helmet and his joints creak as he stands to attention.

"I am at your service." The metallic voice echoes around the chamber.

Heston steps forward and repeats the line loudly and slowly but the knight replies instantly, "I already serve somebody. I cannot have two masters."

Heston slides down onto his bottom and starts to sob loudly. Gloria pats you on the back and says "Very clever! Now what will you make him do?"

"Make him throw Heston onto the moon!" Colin says cheerfully.

The Magic Knight

You think long and hard before deciding on the best command of all. "Magic Knight, I command you to pick up Heston and escort him to Miss Brimstone's office and explain everything that he did. After that, I command you to never obey another person again. You are free! I recommend you go on a long holiday!"

The Magic Knight bows deeply before picking Heston up by his collar. He turns to face you and says, "Don't worry, I have a holiday booked in Berlin soon! I shall return to my cabinet to rest as soon I have dealt this with wretched thing." The knight nods and walks away, the poor boy's feet dangle and swing in the air as he tries to wiggle free. The two of them are soon lost in the darkness of the caves.

Go to **8**

The Magic Knight

36

You push open the trapdoor and clamber up the last few steps into the chilly room above. You breathe a sigh of relief that you've finally managed to find a well-used room. You look around for the others but are frozen solid by a screeching voice from the other side of the room.

"And just what are you doing breaking into my office?"

You slowly turn around and look sadly into Miss Brimstone's eyes. You sigh heavily and sit yourself down on the hard wooden bench. You know that this detention will be a big one. You just hope that you are out in time for Christmas. **Bad luck, you won't be going anywhere for a while! Game over!**

The Magic Knight

37

Miss Brimstone opens her eyes and stares at you all.

"You are very lucky," she screeches, "that I have better things to do than sort out your little mistakes. Whatever hogwash you may choose to believe, the real thief is getting away and so, please, stop wasting my time."

You sense that you are off the hook and quickly race out of Miss Brimstone's office and into the hallway. You turn around to ask Gloria what she thinks might have happened to the knight but she is already racing down the steps that lead to the bottom of the tower.

Go to **92**

The Magic Knight

38

You suck the leaf and wince as a bitter juice squirts onto your tongue. It tastes like old boots mixed with warm lemon. Nevertheless, you can soon feel your body grow lighter and you realise that you aren't sitting on the branch any more, you are floating an inch above it.

Holding your breath, you push yourself away from the wall and are relieved to find that you still float. You discover that you can swim through the air like water though you can only go downwards, the leaf was clearly not strong enough to let you float upwards.

Not wanting to risk the effects wearing off halfway up the tower, you quickly make your way down to the

The Magic Knight

ground and dust yourself off as Gloria brings Trixie and Colin down to join you.

Go to **110**

39

You follow the stair case down further into the hill. The steps seem endless and you start to worry about how slippery they are becoming. You place your foot forwards onto a wooden step and try to pull back as it snaps under your weight. You aren't quick enough though and you fall forwards and land heavily on your back on a pile of loose stone. You start to slide uncontrollably down the shale until you bump to a halt against a wooden door.

Through the door you can hear muffled noises so you nervously push

The Magic Knight

it open. Gloria, Colin and Trixie spin round and look surprised to see you.

"I guess you found a secret way into the room!" Gloria chuckles. "Never mind, you're here now!"

You join your friends in the room. Go to **63**

40

You don't have time to react and feel the magic hit you and a sudden sensation of shrinking very quickly and your legs growing longer. When you look down you realise with horror that you have been turned into a frog!

It looks like your first day at Monstacademy hasn't gone to plan and you hop off to find a teacher to turn you back into your normal self.

The Magic Knight

For now, it looks like you won't be solving the mystery of the Magic Knight. Bad luck! Game over!

41

Luckily you are able to reach up and scratch your itchy ear without disturbing Gloria's grip on your collar and you are glad when you can feel solid ground underneath your feet again. You sit down on a cold stone and watch as Gloria travels back up and down the tower bringing Trixie and then Colin down to join you.

Go to **110**

42

You add four flakes of baboon dandruff to the potion and it seems to be working well. It turns gloriously

The Magic Knight

clear and has lots of small bubbles, like the finest champagne. Heston takes a spoon and offers some to Kevin to taste. You suddenly realise that if you take three apples from the table, you end up with three apples, not four!

You knock the spoon away before he can drink it but some of it splashes onto your face and drips down onto your lips. Before you can think it through, your tongue darts out and licks it up. It tastes like chicken soup.

Suddenly your whole body starts tickling and you fall about in fits of giggles. Through the tears in your eyes you see Heston and his friends backing out of the door before locking it behind them.

You don't have time to worry about

The Magic Knight

them though as the tickling starts to get even worse. You realise that you have no idea how you will make it through a day of this; that is, if it even wears off after a day!

For now, though, you accept that you are stuck in the storeroom alone and giggling. **Your situation is no laughing matter but it definitely looks like your first day at Monstacademy has come to a bad end! Bad luck! Game over!**

43

You head over to the museum only to find it closed for lunch. The door is unlocked though and you wonder whether to sneak in to take a look. Colin thinks that having a look now would be a great idea but Gloria and Trixie are more cautious.

The Magic Knight

To open the door and take a look, go to **4**

To head to Miss Flopsbottom's office go to **81**

44

You add two troll's bogeys to the clear potion and stand back as a tower of thick, dark smoke erupts from the cauldron and leaves a big black mark on the ceiling. As you watch, the potion starts to thicken up and turn a mustard-yellow colour with brown lumps floating to the surface.

Mr Snickletinkle wanders over and pulls a large silver spoon from behind his ear. As quick as a flash he dips it into the potion and pours a small drop into his mouth. Suddenly, he hiccups, his eyes cross and he looks confused. Then, without warning, a

The Magic Knight

loud raspberry sound erupts from his bottom. Mr Snickletinkle tries his best to cover the sounds with his hands but it's no good. Every time he takes a step it sounds like somebody is stepping on an angry duck.

Eventually the teacher runs from the room and the class breaks out into fits of laughter. Miss Brimstone hears the noise and storms in through the open door. Heston is all too happy to fill her in on the details and she drags you and your friends off to her office for a very long detention.

Go to **22**

45

When you arrive at the library you find it deserted. There is a handwritten sign on the librarian's

The Magic Knight

desk that says "Gone to lunch".

Immediately behind the librarian's desk is the roped off area that is filled with books that cover topics of Dark Monsterology. You know that this area is off-limits to all students until they are in their fourth year but you also know that this is where the information that you need is most likely to be found.

You all decide that you need to sneak into the out-of-bounds Dark Section and that you'll need somebody to stand guard. You instantly all look at Colin but he whines and moans about the fact that he's always chosen for guard duty.

To stand guard yourself and let the others sneak into the dark section go to **66**

The Magic Knight

To force Colin to stand guard and sneak in with the others go to **102**

46

You carefully climb down the wooden steps, sliding down on your bottom where needed and breath a huge sigh of relief when you finally reach a cold, draughty room. A pair of cold hands grab you from behind and you hear a familiar voice in your ear.

"Gotcha!"

You laugh and slap Colin's hands away. You are so glad to see them that you can't stay mad at him for making you jump.

You look around and your heart sinks as you realise that you are in a circular room with solid stone walls all

The Magic Knight

the way round.

Gloria smiles and whistles a funny little tune. With a slow grinding sound, part of the stone wall starts to slide backwards revealing a hidden doorway into a well-lit room beyond.

"Learned that in a book as well?" Colin asks with a smirk. Gloria looks embarrassed but says nothing.

You follow the others through the doorway. Go to **29**

47

It takes you a while to scrape all of the troll's bogeys out of the bottom of the jar but eventually you've added enough. As you add the last one the clear potion starts to fizz before thickening up and changing to a thick, lumpy, vomit-coloured soup.

The Magic Knight

Viscous bubbles pop on the surface and the smell of rotten pigeon poo fills the classroom. You pull your shirt over your nose to try to keep the worst of the stench out but it still makes you feel sick.

Mr Snickletinkle rushes over to your desk with a big smile on his face. "The best potions always smell the worst!" he says with glee. He pulls a large silver soup spoon from his pocket and brushes off a few specks of dust. He scoops up a big dollop of the soup and swallows it whole. For a moment nothing happens. Then, one by one, the old vampire's bones start to turn to jelly. First to go are his arms which flop by his side. Then his legs crumple underneath him and finally his skull. He seems perfectly fine in himself and you hear him muttering from the floor. "I say!

The Magic Knight

You appear to have made a bone-destabilising potion! Jolly good show! Though I do appear to have turned into something similar to a blob fish! I know how a jellyfish feels now and no mistake!"

You start to apologise but the teacher waves you away. "Don't be silly! We all make mistakes. If you wouldn't mind fetching Miss Brimstone though, I'm sure she'll put me right."

Just as he is mentioning her name, the deputy-headmistress storms through the door as if she was summoned by magic. She takes one look at the floppy Mr Snickletinkle and drags you and your friends out of the classroom by the scruff of your neck. Leaving Mr Snickletinkle on the floor, she marches you away to her office for a very long detention.

Go to **22**

48

The curator explains that the Magic Knight has been one of the more popular exhibits in recent years and that the *Museum der monströsen Freuden*, or Museum of Monstrous Delights, in Berlin has asked to borrow it for a while to include in an exhibition. He tells you that the suit of armour was due to be carefully packed tomorrow but that, unless it can be found quickly, he will have to tell the Germans that there is no suit of armour to borrow.

Go to **113**

49

Trixie sits down next to the Magic

The Magic Knight

Knight and puts her arm around his shoulder. "You know *why* they want you to go to Berlin, don't you?" she asks. The knight shrugs his shoulders so Trixie continues. "They are terribly worried over there about their magical artifacts being stolen. They have heard what an amazing job you've done here and that not a single thing has ever been stolen whilst you've been on watch."

"This is true I suppose." The knight sniffs loudly.

"Only, the thing is…" Trixie trails off.

"What? What's the thing?" The knight seems suddenly very curious.

"Well, right now, something *has* been stolen, hasn't it? At least, everyone thinks that it has."

The Magic Knight

The knight seems to think for a moment before making up his mind. His joints creak as he pushes himself to his feet and he leans forward and gives Trixie a big hug.

"You are right." he says in his metallic voice. "I shall go and find Miss Flopsbottom and explain everything. I need to clear my name! I shall enjoy my time in Berlin and make sure that nothing is stolen whilst I am there. Thank you!"

Trixie smiles and gives you a wink as the Magic Knight disappears back along the corridor.

"Come on," Colin says cheerfully. "it's lunch time!"

You laugh and realise that, even though you haven't been at Monstacademy for long, you are

The Magic Knight

going to enjoy it here.

Congratulations, you've solved the mystery of the Magic Knight!

50

It doesn't seem like your friends have been gone for long when you hear the sound of the librarian returning from her lunch. You have heard that the librarian is a fierce stone gargoyle and you can definitely hear the tip-tap rhythm of her stone feet tapping against the stone floor.

You think quickly and decide your only hope is to distract her before she discovers your plan and punishes you all. On top of the desk is a cricket ball, obviously confiscated from some unfortunate child in the past. You pick it up and look around. To your left there are dozens of tall racks of

The Magic Knight

books heading into the distance. You realise that if you can throw the ball to the other side of the racks, the librarian may be distracted enough to go and check out the noise.

You weigh the ball in your hand and throw it as hard as you can.

Roll a dice.

If you roll a 1, 2, 3 or 4, go to **30**

If you roll a 5 or 6, go to **105**

51

Well done! You made your first decision! Even though you soon end up lost and wandering the corridors looking for your first lesson, Miss Flopsbottom, the headmistress, soon finds you and compliments you on your perfect school uniform.

The Magic Knight

She reminds you that you are late for your first history lesson and helpfully points you in the right direction and tells you to hurry along. She offers to take your bags up to your room so that you don't have to rush around quite as much.

You rush off to find the history classroom at the bottom of the tallest tower. Go to **121**

52

A sketch of the footprints is great but you realise that you need to know for sure if they match those of the Magic Knight.

You decide that the library is the best place to go as they will definitely have more information. Go to **45**

The Magic Knight

__53__

You try to flick the potion over Heston and Kevin and most of it does fly out of the bottle and land on their heads. Unfortunately, some of the potion dribbles out of the bottle as you are shaking it and lands straight on your nose. It tickles your nostril and you react by sniffing hard, forgetting that this will suck the potion up into your nose!

As you feel every part of your body freeze solid you at least feel good about the fact that Heston won't be executing his evil plan any time soon.

For now, though, you are stuck in the storeroom with Heston and his friends. **You never imagined your first day at Monstacademy would end in such a sticky situation! Bad luck! Game over!**

The Magic Knight

54

You follow Heston a little further but as soon as he and his friends disappear round a corner you spin around and race off in the opposite direction. You run back past the history classroom and catch up with Trixie and her friends soon after.

You apologise to them all for rushing up on them but that you had decided to leave with Heston and soon learned that it was a big mistake. You tell them about his secret storeroom and how it just sounded like too much trouble.

Trixie and her friends laugh and Trixie says, "He definitely is trouble. He tried to poison the entire town of Wexbridge not so long ago, you are definitely better off with us!"

The Magic Knight

Relieved that you've made the right choice, you follow Trixie and her friends towards the main hall. Go to **20**

55

Gloria is quicker at Latin than you and blurts out "Forget your master. Follow me?"

"Indeed." Miss Brimstone enters the room through yet another hidden door. "Heston, did you really think that the King who created this magical wonder didn't think to protect himself in case his enemies took it hostage? I'm disappointed in you."

Miss Flopsbottom coughs quietly and says, "Miss Brimstone, I trust that you can escort Mr Gobswaddle back to your office to await his

The Magic Knight

punishment? I would quite like a word with our heroes." Miss Brimstone nods curtly and drags Heston out through the secret doorway. The Magic Knight follows after them. As he's about to leave, he says, "Thank you all for saving me. I think I shall return to my cabinet for a rest. After all, I have a holiday in Berlin to look forward to!"

You laugh and turn back to Miss Flopsbottom. The headmistress says, "Thank you all for solving this mystery for us. Never tell her that I told you this, but the only reason Miss Brimstone knew to look for you here was because she returned to her office to collect something and realised that you had escaped your detention. She was very impressed, and that doesn't happen often!" You blush along with your

The Magic Knight

friends. "Anyway, in honour of your achievements, let me present you with these." Miss Flopsbottom leans forward and places a large gold medal hung on a silver ribbon over your head. "These are awarded to students of Monroe's Academy who show great bravery and intelligence. I can't think of any children more deserving!"

You smile and hug Colin, Gloria and Trixie. You realise that, even though you haven't been at Monstacademy for long, you are going to enjoy it here!

Congratulations, you've solved the mystery of the Magic Knight!

56

Throughout your time at Monstacademy you may find that you

The Magic Knight

have to make a decision. Sometimes this is something that you can choose yourself and sometimes you will be asked to roll a dice to decide what happens (just like you did when you decided what type of monster you are).

Be warned though, not all decisions are good decisions. Some will change the way the story goes and some will lead you off in dangerous directions. Some may lead to dead ends and some may mean that the story ends right there and then, often with a long detention! The only way you can complete the story with a happy ending is to make sure you make the best decisions that you can and try to solve the mystery of the Magic Knight!

Let's have a go at making another

The Magic Knight

decision now. For your first day at Monstacademy, do you wear your white trainers or your black shoes?

For white trainers, go to **75**

For black shoes, go to **51**

57

You close your eyes and turn into a bat with a pop. You fly up to the ceiling and cling to the roof. As you hang there you watch Miss Brimstone and Heston enter and stand by the door. You look across the room and see Gloria hanging from the light fitting and Colin perched on the windowsill. Heston is trying his hardest to look around but Miss Brimstone is holding him back. "It is incredibly rude to snoop around somebody's office when they are not here! We can clearly see that

The Magic Knight

the room is empty!" she grumbles as she escorts the wailing boy out of the room and locks the door behind them.

You decide to have a quick look around the room before leaving. Go to **28**

58

The red door appears to be magical and as you approach it swings open on its own. Curious, you step through into an almost entirely empty room. On the floor is a scrap of old, stained paper. In faded letters is a message.

I am an odd number. If you take away a single letter, I become even.

You look confused for a while before it starts to make sense. You write down the answer and decide what to

The Magic Knight

do next.

To enter another door, go to **122**

When you are ready to enter the code, go to **89**

59

You ignore your aching legs and climb the staircase. It seems to go on forever but eventually you reach the top. There are two doorways in front of you.

To walk through the doorway on the left, go to **33**

To walk through the doorway on the right, go to **26**

60

Heston throws the book against the wall and storms over to the Magic

The Magic Knight

Knight. "Just do what I tell you metal man otherwise I'll let you rust at the bottom of the ocean!"

By a lucky coincidence, those are the exact words needed to get the Magic Knight to follow your every command and the suit of armour jolts to its feet and stands to attention. "I am yours to command, master." The hollow, metallic voice seems more determined now.

Heston can't believe his luck and starts dancing around in circles, whooping and hollering. "Spin Trixie around over your head!" he yells. The knight reaches out and grabs your friend by her dress and hoists her up over his head like a weight lifter. He starts spinning in a slow circle but soon gets faster and faster until poor Trixie is nothing but a blur. Her

The Magic Knight

screams sound strange at such a high speed.

Eventually the knight grinds to a halt and places Trixie onto her feet. She promptly falls over dizzy and throws up into Heston's hat that he has placed on the floor out of the way.

"I have all the power! The world is mine to control!" The young wizard is red with excitement now.

"Not quite!" The shrill shriek causes you to spin around even though you know that only one person could speak with such anger. *"Dominus obliviscar tui. Sequi me."*

Go to **55**

The Magic Knight

61

You decide that you don't want to be a thief and place the key back onto the desk. You get comfortable in the chair and wait patiently for your friends to return.

Go to **50**

62

Well done! You realise that if you take three apples from the table then you end up with three apples, the other one is still on the table!

You mix the potion up and Heston gives a spoonful to Dilbert to try. He tells him not to worry as he's a ghost anyway so it can't do him any harm. Dilbert takes the medicine and instantly freezes solid like a perfectly formed statue.

The Magic Knight

Heston laughs out loud and mutters about how rich and powerful he's going to be. He starts to pour the potion into bottles ready to take down to the big fridge that holds all of the food and drink for the school. If he manages to get the potion into the milk and juice, the whole school will be frozen solid before they can do anything about it!

You realise that you can't let Heston get away with this and you decide to do something quickly.

To run away to find a teacher to tell, go to **9**

To pick up a bottle of potion to throw at Heston and Kevin go to **108**

63

You step forwards into the secret

The Magic Knight

room. There are torches burning around the walls and three doors leading off at different angles. One of the doors is painted bright red, another dark green and a third is buttercup yellow.

To the right of the door are three discs with the numbers 1 to 9 painted around the edges. Each disc is painted to match the colour of one of the doors. There is a metal arrow hammered into the wall above each one.

"It's like a lock!" Trixie squeals as she runs over to the wheels and starts turning them. "Look, we need to enter the correct code and I bet another door will open!"

"How do we know what the code is smarty-pants?" asks Colin grumpily.

The Magic Knight

"I bet they are behind the doors. I bet the number for the red disc is behind the red door and so on."

"I think she's right." says Gloria. "Besides, we've not got any better ideas. This wasn't on the map that I saw."

Go to **122**

The Magic Knight

64

You duck under the desk just in time to hear Miss Brimstone and Heston enter the office. You can hear Heston trying to snoop around but Miss Brimstone isn't letting him out of her sight.

"There is clearly nobody in here," she argues. "I'm not sure why you are insisting on wasting my time but it stops now!"

Despite Heston's protests, you hear the two of them leave the room and lock the door behind them. You crawl out from under the desk and watch as Trixie comes out from the wardrobe, Colin hops down from the window sill and Gloria flies down from the roof. You all agree that this was a narrow escape but you decide to have

The Magic Knight

a quick look around the room before leaving. Go to **28**

65

You get to the museum in time to see a small man, made almost entirely out of a shiny stone, opening the door. "He's a troll." Gloria whispers. "He's the curator as well."

The troll asks if there is anything that he can help you with?

If you have a **Flier** in your backpack, go to **113**

Otherwise go to **48**

66

Even though you volunteered you are not happy at being forced to stay outside and keep guard. You sit down at the librarian's desk and put your

The Magic Knight

feet up onto the table. You stretch your leg out and a loud *clunk* breaks the silence as you knock an old keyring onto the flagstones.

You reach down and pick it up. There is a single key and a handwritten paper tag that says "Master Key". The key glistens as you look at it and appears to change shape depending on the angle that you hold it. Sometimes it is an old-fashioned brass key best suited for locking a garden gate and at others a small silver key better suited to opening a delicate locket.

To keep the set of keys for yourself, go to **15**

To put the keys back onto the desk, go to **61**

The Magic Knight

67

The first thing you notice as you enter the next room is a single candle flickering on top of a wooden stool. It has nearly burnt down to the nub. Behind the candle, sat hugging his knees to his chest, is the Magic Knight. He is slumped so low that he is nearly lying down and he looks more like a pile of scrap metal. When you look closer you see that his shoulders are jumping up and down and a soft whimper is coming from inside the helmet.

You walk closer and put your arm around him and ask what is wrong.

"They want to get rid of me!" he wails in an echoing, metallic voice. "I've been in this castle for hundreds of years and now they want to send

The Magic Knight

me away to Berlin! I'm not wanted!"

Colin steps forward and offers the knight his dirty handkerchief. The knight takes it and blows something like his nose. He continues to whine. "I tried to tell Miss Flopsbottom how I was feeling. I felt bad when I ran away and saw all the chaos that it caused so I went to her office to tell but she'd already left to explain it to the Grand High Monster! I'm going to be in so much trouble." The Magic Knight starts to sob loudly again.

Gloria pulls you all over to one side for a private chat. Go to **100**

68

You carefully drop the troll's bogeys in to the cauldron and take a quick step back as it starts to shake and rattle on the desk. It seems like

The Magic Knight

something big is about to happen and you all duck behind your stools. Suddenly, a giant bubble rises to the surface of the clear liquid and pops with a loud GLOOP, and that's it. The potion is now a dark, midnight blue but nothing more appears to be happening.

Mr Snickletinkle makes his way over to the desk and pulls a tarnished silver spoon out of his chest pocket. He licks his lips and scoops up a small portion of the runny liquid. He lets it slide over his lips and gargles it for a while. Nothing seems to happen. He certainly isn't about to go flying off amongst the clouds. Then, as slowly as an iceberg crashing into a cliff, the teacher's face starts to turn bright beetroot red.

He opens his mouth wide as if he

The Magic Knight

is about to scream but no sound comes out. He hiccups. And then it happens. A bright yellow flame shoots from the back of his throat like an enormous dragon and flies across the table where it lands on Esme Furfang. Unfortunately, Esme is a werewolf and the flame sets the hairs on her head on fire. One of her friends, thinking quick on their feet, throws a glass of water over her and Esme just stands there sizzling and grumbling. She stamps her feet and storms out of the classroom, her smoking head making her look like a furious steam train.

Just as Esme storms out of the door, Miss Brimstone storms into the classroom demanding to know what all of the fuss is about. She sees Mr Snickletinkle hiccupping fire and realises at once that you and your

The Magic Knight

friends are to blame. Grabbing you by your ears she marches you off to her office for a very long detention.

Go to **22**

69

Miss Brimstone continues to shout at you until she is hoarse and your ears hurt. Eventually she stops and takes a deep breath. "I cannot trust you children to be loose in the school whilst we have such an important and serious breach of security. Until we solve this case and the suit of armour turns up, you will spend your time locked in my office away from the rest of the children. Follow me!"

The deputy-headmistress leads you away to her office, muttering under her breath about how rude and reckless you have been. **It looks**

The Magic Knight

like you won't be doing anything more until the suit of armour is found. Bad luck! Game over!

70

The cellar is chilly when you finally make it. You all sit down on the cold, stone floor and gather around the large book.

Gloria quickly thumbs through the pages until she finds the section marked for the Magic Knight. Underneath the big title is a beautifully detailed sketch of what you assume is the suit of armour. You read through the information and learn that the Magic Knight once served the ancient kings of England and it was used to help them defeat the kings of Europe. Over time, it became nothing more than a legend

The Magic Knight

and eventually it was lost in a keep or cellar in some forgotten castle.

There is nothing to confirm that the suit of armour found its way to Monstacademy though and you all realise that you will need to find even more information before you can be sure.

If you have a **Sketch of the Footprints** in your backpack, go to **34**

Otherwise, go to **95**

71

You thank your lucky stars that you chose the stronger steps. You take them two at a time and soon reach the top. There is a wooden trapdoor covering a hole in the roof but it doesn't appear to be locked.

The Magic Knight

To open the trapdoor, go to **36**

To head back down, go to **26**

72

You get dressed for bed and pull back the heavy duvet on your four-poster bed. You watch as the various monsters crawl into their baskets or hang from the ceiling or even climb up onto the roof and wish that you had a more exciting bed. You've tried your best and your parents have even bought you a duvet cover designed to look like a stone crypt but it's not quite the same.

After a while, you fall asleep worrying about who stole the magical suit of armour and what on Earth they plan to do with it. Go to **126**

The Magic Knight

73

You head over to Miss Flopsbottom's office only to find the door locked. You all decide that you definitely need to speak to her but, if she's not here, then maybe having a quick look in her office could help you out.

If you have a **Master Key** in your backpack go to **6**

Otherwise go to **83**

74

Miss Brimstone continues to tell you off. "Despite how rude you have been; it is very important that you hear what Miss Flopsbottom has to say. Get back into the hall and be sure to keep your mouths closed until you are spoken to."

The Magic Knight

Sheepishly, you sneak back into the hall and take your seats to listen to the headmistress. Go to **119**

<u>75</u>

Well done! You made your first decision! You've decided to wear your white trainers to your first day at school. Unfortunately, as you are wandering around the corridors lost and confused, the headmistress, Miss Flopsbottom, catches you and forces you to change into your black shoes. Bad luck!

You look at your timetable and realise that you are already late for your first history lesson. You don't want to make a bad impression on your first day, you're already nervous enough.

You throw your bags into your new

The Magic Knight

room and rush off to find the history classroom. All you know is that it's at the bottom of the tallest tower. Go to **121**

76

You sprint along the dark passageway making sure to concentrate on the uneven floor. You soon realise that you are running in a long, winding circle and, before you know it, you are back outside the door to Miss Flopsbottom's office. In the distance you can hear Miss Brimstone scolding Heston for wasting her time as they walk away.

You walk up to the door and find that it is still locked.

If you have a **Master Key** in your backpack, go to **6**

The Magic Knight

Otherwise, go to **83**

77

You race along the corridor to Miss Flopsbottom's office and bump into the caretaker, Grimsby. You explain that you are looking for Miss Flopsbottom but he tells you that she has already left to visit the Grand High Monster to give him the bad news of the theft.

Grimsby looks sad and tells you that Miss Flopsbottom is worried that this could be the end of Monstacademy, unless the suit of armour is found quickly. You start to panic and promise that you will do anything you can to help find it. You ask where it is normally kept and Grimsby tells you that it has always been kept on display in the school

The Magic Knight

museum and that was where it was stolen from.

Colin points out that a visit to the museum would be a good idea to find out more but Trixie and Gloria want to try Miss Flopsbottom's office first.

To go visit the museum, go to **43**

To go to Miss Flopsbottom's office, go to **81**

78

You take a deep breath and head off down the corridor. This one seems longer than the others and the floor slowly rises higher and higher as you get further and further along it. After a while, you find yourself at another dead end, only this one is blocked by a wooden door.

The Magic Knight

Hoping that it is the history classroom or that somebody on the other side can at least help, you push it open and step inside.

Go to **125**

79

You can feel the ground rising up under your feet and your legs start to ache as you climb the slop. After a short while you arrive at two staircases. One leads upwards and the other down.

To head upwards, go to **59**

To head downwards, go to **39**

80

You carefully make your way around Miss Flopsbottom's office trying hard not to disturb anything.

The Magic Knight

Most of the shelves are filled with dog-eared books and memorabilia from various holidays. On one shelf there is a giant sea-shell with the words "Welcome to Blackpool! The Costa Del Sol of the North!" picked out in tacky beads.

None of the others have any more luck in their searches and so you move over to Miss Flopsbottom's desk. You daren't look through her chest of drawers, that would be going too far, but you do notice something unusual on the floor just in front of it. Like everywhere else in the office, there is a layer of dust on the floor and you notice that a pair of large, pointy feet have left a recent impression in it. They definitely look like the sort of footprints a suit of armour would leave but you ask yourself why the Magic Knight

The Magic Knight

would be stood in front of Miss Flopsbottom's desk if he had been stolen?

"You don't think Miss Flopsbottom would..." Colin trails off, the thought is too ridiculous to consider.

"She has been under a lot of stress lately." Gloria offers. "Maybe she thought she could sell it and retire on a desert island somewhere?"

"Or maybe she snapped and wants to take over the world!" Colin adds a little too enthusiastically. He grabs a piece of paper from Miss Flopsbottom's desk and sketches the footprints, making sure to get the correct size and shape. **Add a Sketch of the Footprints to your backpack.**

If you have **Monstrous and**

The Magic Knight

Magical Artifacts Vol. III in your backpack, go to **31**

Otherwise go to **52**

81

You find your way to Miss Flopsbottom's office but the door is locked. Just as you are trying to open the door, Heston Gobswaddle and his cronies stumble into the corridor and see what you are doing. Heston is convinced that you are trying to break in to the headmistress's office to steal something and he runs off to try to find a teacher.

To try to enter the office, go to **112**

To run and try to escape, go to **99**

82

"Well my dear, lost already?" You

The Magic Knight

spin around and see Miss Brimstone, the deputy-headmistress and a banshee, and breathe a sigh of relief. At least you are safe now.

She hands you a map of the school and tells you to keep hold of it for next time. **Add the Map of the School to your backpack**.

Miss Brimstone leads you gently by your arm back along another corridor that looks identical to the others and, before long, you find yourself in the doorway to your history lesson. The deputy-headmistress gives you a nod and leaves you alone to find a seat amongst all of your classmates.

Go to **84**

83

You realise that the only way you

The Magic Knight

are going to be able to look inside Miss Flopsbottom's office is if you pick the lock.

Roll a dice.

If you roll an even number go to **94**

If you roll an odd number go to **14**

84

It looks like the lesson has already started when you slip quietly through the classroom door so you quickly grab the closest free stool and take a seat at the table. At the front of the class an Egyptian mummy is droning on about the Third Dynasty of Egypt and how it was so much better than all of the other Dynasties that followed after (back then Egyptian children really respected their elders and didn't run in the hallways like

The Magic Knight

Fourth Dynasty Egyptian children did).

You look around at your new classmates. On your left is an ugly little boy with a scrunched up, angry face and a too-small wizard's hat pulled down over his ears. He introduces himself as Heston Gobswaddle in a nasal, whiny voice and says that he is the person to know at Monstacademy. Apparently all of the teachers are scared of his dad so he can do whatever he likes.

On your right is a red-headed girl who looks almost as nervous as you. She is chattering away to a vampire and a hairy boy who is most likely a werewolf. She notices you staring at her and gives you a little wave. She introduces herself as Trixie Grimble. The boy gives you a hairy grin and

The Magic Knight

tries to high-five you but misses and smacks the vampire on the head. She gives him a stern telling off.

All of a sudden, the class is disturbed by Miss Flopsbottom, the headmistress, bursting through the doors, storming to the front of the class and clapping her hands together noisily.

It is hard to understand her because she keeps stopping and starting and changing what it is that she's saying. From what you can tell, a ceremonial suit of armour has been stolen from the museum and all students are to report to the main hall immediately.

Excited by this turn of events, the other children start to scrabble for their bags and head for the door. On

The Magic Knight

your way out, you notice Trixie and Heston heading in opposite directions. You're not sure where the main hall is yet and really don't want to get lost again so soon after last time. You decide to follow either Heston or Trixie to make sure.

To follow Heston, go to **27**

To follow Trixie, go to **20**

85

Oh dear! You add a single flake of baboon dandruff to the potion, forgetting that the riddle asked you how many apples **you** had. If you took three apples, you would have three. The one apple would be left on the table!

Suddenly the potion starts to bubble and turn a sludgy brown

The Magic Knight

colour. Heston looks angry as he scoops up a spoonful and pushes it towards your mouth to try. It doesn't matter how much you resist, he soon gets enough on your lips to taste and then it happens. You feel your arms growing to three times their normal length whilst your legs shrink until they are the same size as those of a sausage dog. No matter how hard you try to run away, you keep tripping over your arms. Heston just laughs as he runs through the door and locks it behind him.

You fall into a corner and hope that the effects will still wear off after a day. **It's unlikely that you'll feel the long arm of the law for your mistake but your first day at Monstacademy has definitely come up short! Bad luck!**

The Magic Knight

86

Taking the left passageway, you see a light ahead and pick up your speed until you are nearly jogging. As you get close you realise it is a group of fireflies huddled together against the rock. You step in for a closer look and don't notice the slope in the ground. You slip onto your back and slide down the loose dirt until you find yourself in a familiar passageway.

Go to **97**

87

You get dressed for bed and pull back the curtain that surrounds your coffin. Some vampires like to sleep hanging from the ceiling like a bat, some of the more traditional ones prefer to sleep in an old coffin. Your mother and father have always

The Magic Knight

insisted on following the old ways and have insisted that you bring your coffin along from home. You settle in to the comfortable cushions and close your eyes and start to go over the events of the day.

You fall asleep worrying about who might possibly want a magical suit of armour and what they plan to do with it. Go to **126**

88

The lock clicks open but it's a second too late and Miss Brimstone bursts round the corner with a gleeful Heston at her heels.

"See! I told you they were trying to break into Miss Flopsbottom's office!" Heston shouts with obvious delight.

You are so ashamed that you

The Magic Knight

can't even hear the words as Miss Brimstone screams and shouts at you about how serious a crime this is and how badly you have let both yourself and Monstacademy down. The only words that filter through are "... permanently expelled!"

When you started Monstacademy yesterday, you never expected to be expelled so soon. Unfortunately, it looks like you won't be spending any more time solving the mystery of the Magic Knight. Bad luck! Game over!

89

"It's no good." Trixie says with frustration. "We can't crack the code."

"Don't worry. I've found it!" you

The Magic Knight

say excitedly.

You step forwards and look at the discs. The first disc is yellow, the second is green and the third is red. You slowly turn the yellow disc until it is at the correct number. Then, you rotate the green disc until it is lined up and finally you move on to the red disc. This one is a little rusty and it takes more effort to get it to spin but you soon have the metal arrow pointed at the correct number.

To find out if you have the correct code, go to the code number that you have entered (top tip: keep your finger on this page in case you are wrong!).

If the code you entered wasn't correct and you've found your way back here, go to **122** to try again!

The Magic Knight

90

It doesn't take long before you are stumbling over roots in the ground and hitting your head on low rocks. Gloria and Colin are finding it easy to find their way in the dark and Trixie seems much more comfortable than you but you push on anyway desperately trying to keep up.

You don't see a sharp rock hanging from the ceiling and you hit your head against it and fall to the ground. By the time you have come to your senses again, the rest of the group have disappeared into the darkness. You try hard not to panic and crawl on into the growing darkness.

Go to **97**

The Magic Knight

91

You are a vampire! You have given up on sucking human blood though and now only drink the blood of cows, pigs and, for some reason, badgers. You love badger blood!

You also have the ability to read people's minds but that's not something that will win you many friends so you might be best to keep that to yourself!

Good luck with your first day at Monstacademy. Go to **56**

92

You race down the steps after Gloria and are shocked when she doesn't stop at the door out into the main school. Instead she ducks under the "No Entry" sign and carries on

The Magic Knight

heading downwards. You soon start to feel dizzy and slow down a little. You don't really want to descend the rest of the stairs head-first.

Eventually, Gloria stops heading downwards and you catch up with her. You wonder if the only reason she has stopped is because she ran out of down. Despite there being no more steps, there doesn't seem to be any other point to the round room that you find yourself in. There are no doors or furniture, it is just a bare room circled by a cold, stone wall on which two flaming torches were hung. The torches are simple bundles of rags stuffed into metal holders that have been hammered into cracks in between the stones.

"I've seen rooms like this!" shouts Colin, suddenly breaking the silence.

The Magic Knight

"I know what to do!" He steps forward and grabs hold of one of the torches. "This is a secret leaver that opens a hidden door!" He pulls on the torch hard but all that happens is that the metal holder slips out from between the stones and the rags burn the tips of Colin's fingers. "Maybe not..." he mutters as he sucks his fingers.

"You were close," Gloria says kindly. "You just got carried away." She reaches out and pulls the other torch softly. It creaks slowly but, sure enough, it slides easily away from the wall. There is a soft rumble and a section of stones starts to slide slowly inwards revealing a secret doorway into another room.

You step through the doorway. Go to **63**

The Magic Knight

<u>93</u>

You push the green door hard but the hinges are stiff. It takes a lot of effort before it finally grinds open and reveals the room beyond.

In the middle of the floor is a stone plinth with the words "HOW MUCH IS LEFT?" scratched onto the front face. On top of the plinth are five pots, each a different size. The biggest is filled with water and has the number 10 written on the front in chalk. The other four are empty and have the numbers 1, 2, 3 and 4 written on the front. You look hard at the jugs for a while before realising what the answer is. You write it down and decide what to do next.

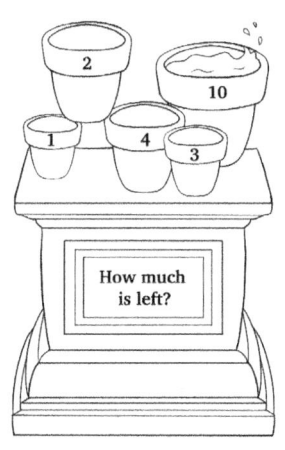

To enter another door, go to **122**

To enter the code, go to **89**

The Magic Knight

94

It takes you a while but eventually you manage to use one of Gloria's hair grips to pick the lock. The door swings open silently and you make your way inside, making sure to lock the door behind you with the keys on Miss Flopsbottom's desk.

Go to **80**

95

You all decide that you can't be sure yet if it is the same suit of armour in the book or something completely different. You throw the book into your backpack and decide to head off to find more information.

You all decide to visit Miss Flopsbottom's office. Go to **73**

The Magic Knight

96

You push open the yellow door and it swings easily inwards. On the other side is an empty, square room, bare except for the following pattern scratched into the wall.

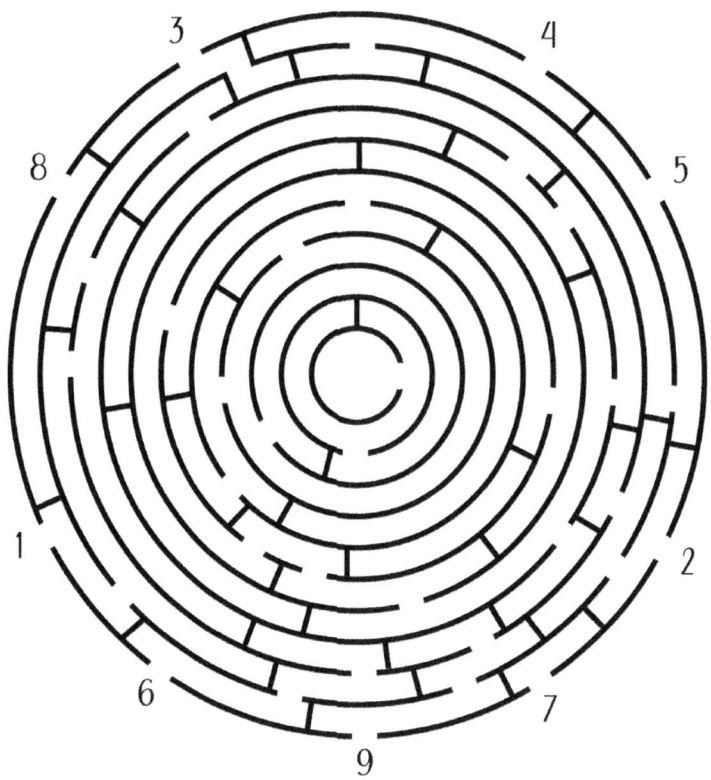

The Magic Knight

It takes you a few minutes to figure out what it means but, as soon as you do, you write the answer down and decide what to do next.

To enter another door, go to **122**

When you are ready to enter the code, go to **89**

97

You arrive at a fork in the passageway.

To take the left passage go to **109**

To take the right passage go to **120**

98

You remember the magical key that you found on the desk in the library and pull it out. You hold it to the lock and watch as it changes shape. Now

The Magic Knight

it looks like a twisted and rusty old key that would crumble to dust as soon as you use it. You place it into the lock and turn it slowly. The lock clicks open and you race through the door as quickly as possible.

Go to **5**

99

You race down the corridor and come to a fork in the passage. To the left is a dark, silent corridor with no lights and a strange sound echoing along it.

To the right is a well-lit corridor. The torches are lit along the wall and you can smell the evening meal being cooked at the other end.

To head to the left, go to **76**

To head to the right, go to **114**

The Magic Knight

100

When she is sure that the Magic Knight can't hear your conversation, Gloria leans in and whispers. "He's a boy, right? We need to appeal to his ego!" She realises that Colin looks confused so explains further. "We need to make him think that it is vitally important that he goes to Berlin. If we do, he might go."

"I think I have an idea." Trixie says. "Leave it to me." She heads back over to the knight. Go to **49**

101

Miss Brimstone opens her eyes and stares at you all.

"What absolute poppycock!" she whispers. "I've heard less nonsense from the moaning monkeys in the

The Magic Knight

library! What's worse is that whilst you have been gallivanting around trying to play detective and wasting my time, the real thief is getting further away! You will stay here until the suit of armour is found!"

The deputy-headmistress storms out of her office and you hear the door lock behind her.

"That's it then!" scowls Colin looking angry.

"Not quite." Gloria says thoughtfully. She wanders over to the big glass window and wiggles the catch until it opens. "I can fly you all down to the ground, just don't look down!" As she says this there is a loud pop and suddenly there is a small black bat flapping around in front of you.

The Magic Knight

Trixie and Colin decide that you should go first and you step up onto the window ledge. You make the mistake of looking down and see that you are so high up that the buildings on the ground look like models. You feel dizzy and have to grab onto the window frame to stop yourself from falling.

You feel Gloria flitting around behind your head and then you feel a small scratch as her tiny feet grip the collar of your uniform. The window ledge seems to drop away as she lifts you effortlessly out into the open and you scream as the ground below drops away.

You try to keep your eyes open as Gloria's wings beat furiously. Annoyingly, the draft of the wings has caused an itch in your ear and you

The Magic Knight

can't help but scratch it.

Roll a dice.

If you roll a 1, 2 or 3, go to **3**

If you roll a 4, 5 or 6, go to **41**

102

You sneak into the darkness with Gloria and Trixie. The books whisper to you in the shadows. Eventually you find a section on magical artifacts but it is hard to see the pages in the darkness.

Gloria finds a big book called Monstrous and Magical Artifacts Vol. III and you decide to take that one away with you. On the floor you find a flier encouraging people to come and look at the magical suit of armour before it is shipped away

The Magic Knight

to spend the next year in a museum in Berlin. **Add the Flier to your backpack.**

Suddenly, you hear Colin whispering that the librarian is on her way back and you head for the door.

You make it out just in time and head down to the cellars to look at it in more detail. **Add Monstrous and Magical Artifacts Vol. III to your backpack.**

Go to **70**

103

You are gifted in the use of magic! You are either a witch or a wizard (I'm sure you can work out which!) and have been able to cast funny spells ever since you were a little child.

The Magic Knight

With great magic comes great responsibility and you are keen to learn just how to control the tingly feelings you get in your fingers whenever you get excited or angry. You don't want another experience like the one at the aquarium involving the octopus, the checkout lady and too much uncontrolled magic!

Good luck with your first day at Monstacademy. Go to **56**

104

Heston soon notices your feet under the curtain and calls Miss Brimstone over to drag you out. The deputy-headmistress yanks open the curtains and you see her face is purple with anger. She doesn't even need to say anything for you to know just how much trouble you are in.

The Magic Knight

When you joined Monstacademy you had no idea you would be expelled so quickly. It looks like you won't be solving the mystery of the Magic Knight today. Bad luck! Game over!

105

Your heart sinks as you watch the tennis ball smash into a glass cabinet full of magical, moaning, monkey heads. With a loud crash, the glass shatters and the monkey heads roll out on to the floor.

You can hear them moaning loudly:

"I say, libraries really have done downhill since I was alive!"

"Monkeys nowadays don't know how to do anything!"

The Magic Knight

"My feet hurt!"

Any hope of escape evaporates as the librarian, an ugly gargoyle, drags herself towards the noise and notices you standing there looking guilty. Without a word, she waves her hands and you suddenly find yourself sat shivering on top of the tallest tower in the school.

You hold on tight to a rusty weathervane and it isn't long before you see Miss Brimstone rise above the clouds on a broomstick ready to take you away for a long detention.

Unfortunately, it looks like you'll be spending the rest of the term hidden away in detention. You won't be solving the mystery of the Magic Knight today! Game over!

The Magic Knight

106

You get down on your hands and knees and take a closer look at the dusty floor. Before you can look too close, you notice a shiny gold coin that has rolled underneath the cabinet. **Congratulations, you found one of the gold coins!**

When you look more closely, you notice that there is a set of familiar footprints in the dust heading away from the cabinet and into the distance. You think to yourself that something as heavy as a suit of armour would need to be dragged away and that this would leave scuffs in the dust, not individual footprints. You explain this to the others and they all look confused, except for Gloria who has a strangely curious look on her face. Before she

The Magic Knight

has chance to explain what she is thinking, the bell rings to signal the start of your next lesson

You all head off to your science lesson. Go to **7**

107

As the last disc slides into place the wall starts to rumble and dust falls down from the ceiling. You all run to take cover on the other side of the chamber as stones start to crumble and slide out of the wall.

Eventually the noise stops and you step through the cloud of dust to see another doorway has opened. Quietly, you all step forward and enter the room beyond.

Go to **67**

The Magic Knight

108

You grab a bottle of the freezing potion and hold it above your head. Heston and Kevin realise what you are planning to do and try to cover their faces. You pull the cork out with a pop and get ready to throw it as hard as you can.

Pick a number between 1 and 10.

For an even number, go to **53**

For an odd number, go to **116**

109

You crawl along the passage to the left and soon realise that you are spiralling up and down and starting to feel dizzy. Before you know it, you are back where you started.

Go to **97**

The Magic Knight

__110__

With another loud pop, Gloria is stood back in front of you looking her usual self. You all start to thank her but she's not listening. She runs away and heads down the hillside to the stream that runs across the field at the base of the tower.

You catch up with her just as she is taking her shoes and socks off and is wading out into the icy water. You quickly kick your shoes off and bundle your socks inside them before jumping in after her.

Gloria soon disappears around a bend in the stream and when you finally catch up with her she is stood at the entrance to a small cave cut into the base of the hill. The stream splashes along just below the

The Magic Knight

entrance and the dirty floor inside is at least dry.

"I had a look at the blueprints to the tower when I was in the Dark Section of the library." Gloria explains to you, Trixie and Colin. "I think this cave leads right underneath and should bring us out into an old storeroom. The Magic Knight was stored there when this castle was first built, I'm wondering if he has returned there for some reason."

"It looks a bit scary in there." you say nervously but none of the others are listening.

"There are a lot of twisty and winding paths in here." Gloria warns you all. "If I remember correctly, you need to head right, right, left, up, right, down and then left. Try not to forget it!" she laughs as you forget it almost immediately.

The vampire tears a strip of cloth from the hem of her dress and wraps it around a bundle of twigs. She strikes a match and soon the rag is burning with a bright glow. Shadows dance up and down the walls but none of the others seem as scared as you. They all stoop down and head into the cave. You don't want to be left on your own and so you step into the darkness after them. Go to **90**

111

Heston pulls the recipe out of his pocket and places it next to the different jars. He reads out the list of ingredients (bat's tongue, the hair of a bald man and the sound of a hyena's laugh, amongst others) but

The Magic Knight

he stops when he gets to baboon's dandruff.

"It doesn't say how much we need." Heston moans. He passes you the book to have a look at and, sure enough, instead of a number there is a riddle to solve. "I bet that's to stop just any old idiot making such a dangerous potion!" he boasts. "I bet we can solve it!"

The riddle says:

There are four apples on a table. You take three. How many apples do you have? The answer will tell you how many flakes of baboon dandruff you should use.

To add one flake, go to **85**

To add three flakes, go to **62**

To add four flakes, go to **42**

The Magic Knight

112

No matter how hard you rattle the handle, the door remains firmly shut. In the distance you can hear Miss Brimstone's shoes clopping along the corridor with Heston ranting and raving in tow.

If you are a witch or wizard go to **32**

If you have a **Master Key** in your backpack go to **98**

If not, **roll a dice.**

If you roll an even number go to **12**

If you roll an odd number go to **88**

113

The curator apologises but says that there is nothing that he can tell

The Magic Knight

you about the knight. He points you in the direction of the cabinet that held the Magic Knight until it was stolen. He says that you are welcome to look around and see if there is any information on the displays that might help.

You walk over to the cabinet to get a better look. Go to **117**

114

You decide to sprint along the well-lit corridor. The glorious smell of food being cooked in the main hall causes your stomach to rumble. Even if you can't find a teacher, you are hopeful that you might find a good meal.

As you round a corner you bump head-first into Miss Brimstone's backside. You send her flying forwards and she lands with a heavy

The Magic Knight

bump on top of a disgruntled Heston Gobswaddle.

"Watch where you are going! You insufferable child!" she screeches as she gets to her feet and dusts herself off. "I'm taking you down to the dungeons to spend some time with Grimsby. He'll have you writing out lines until your eyes go squiffy!"

You sigh and limp along the corridor following behind Miss Brimstone.

Unfortunately, it looks like you will be too busy copying out lines to solve the mystery of the Magic Knight! Bad luck! Game over!

115

You hear Miss Brimstone huff a big sigh and relent to Heston's pressure. She fumbles for her key to the lock

The Magic Knight

and you realise that you have to hide quickly. **Roll a dice.**

If you roll a 1 or 2 you hide behind Miss Flopsbottom's desk. Go to **64**

If you roll a 3 or 4 you hide behind the tall curtains. Go to **23**

If you roll a 5 or 6 you dive inside the big wooden wardrobe. Go to **123**

116

You watch with glee as the potion flies across the room and lands with a splat on Heston and Kevin's face. Within seconds they are frozen solid and only their eyeballs are still moving.

You back out of the storeroom and hear Trixie and her friends at the bottom of the staircase still talking about what Miss Flopsbottom was so worked up about. You sprint to the bottom of the stairs and fall into a heap explaining what has happened and asking if you can hang out with them instead.

They laugh and say they knew Heston was always trouble and welcome you to go with them instead.

Go to **20**

117

You walk over to the tall, glass cabinet and the first thing that you notice is that it is intact. None of the glass panels have even so much as a scratch on them and the lock hasn't been smashed or broken. You think to yourself that surely a burglar would have to break the glass to get the Magic Knight out. There are two other

The Magic Knight

things that catch your eye. There is something odd about the glass door and something unusual on the floor in front of the cabinet.

To look more closely at the glass door, go to **16**

To look more closely at the floor, go to **106**

118

You place the leaves into your mouth and chew them hard. A thick liquid that tastes like a minty liquorish coats the inside of your mouth and throat. Suddenly you start to feel very funny. You start to bob your head up and down and cluck like a chicken. Before you know it you are scratching around on the branch and are convinced that you have wings. This is a bit unfortunate because you

The Magic Knight

haven't actually turned into a chicken and so, with a lurch in your stomach, you step off the branch and start to fall once more towards the ground.

With a jolt you stop falling and feel Gloria's claws on your neck. You hear her shout up to Colin and Trixie that she's got to take you to the nurse's office as quickly as possible. You aren't too worried though, chickens never are! **Your quest to solve the mystery of the Magic Knight has come to an untimely end! Bad luck! Game over!**

119

Miss Brimstone clears her throat and begins to speak loudly and clearly. "Within our school walls we have always been lucky enough to house some of the most majestic and

The Magic Knight

powerful artifacts from throughout history. We have been fortunate to have on display at various times Napoleon Bonaparte's earring, King Henry the Eighth's enchanted necklace that was said to guarantee love to all who wore it and even the magical boxer shorts that once belonged to the King of the Fairies. And until recently we had within our museum a most beautiful and powerful suit of armour. It saddens me to say that this important and indeed very magical artifact has been stolen."

All of the children in the hall start to twitter amongst themselves wondering what its magical powers could be. Eventually, Miss Flopsbottom stands again and the hall falls silent.

The Magic Knight

"Until this suit of armour is found you are all in danger. You shall remain in your rooms during lights out and will be escorted to and from your lessons. Anybody found outside of their rooms without permission will be dealt with severely."

The headmistress sits down and starts fanning her flushed face with her hand. A fourth year student starts to round up the children at your table and you follow him up to your room for the night.

If you are a vampire, go to **87**

If you are a werewolf, go to **19**

If you are a witch or wizard, go to **72**

120

You can hear your friends in the

The Magic Knight

distance and scramble down the passageway until you reach another fork.

To follow the left passage, go to **86**

To follow the right passage, go to **24**

121

It doesn't take long before you are completely and utterly lost. You've managed to find your way into the main school building but there are corridors shooting off in every direction. You follow one after the other but they all seem to lead to dead ends or loop back on themselves.

You suddenly realise that you are lost and alone in a new school filled with monsters. You take a deep

The Magic Knight

breath and remind yourself that you are a monster as well, they are all nice children and the teachers are probably delightful.

Eventually you stop and think. Ahead of you is a long corridor filled with flickering torches and crawling shadows. You realise that you can keep looking or you can accept that you are lost and shout out for help.

To shout for help, go to **82**

To keep going further along the dark corridor go to **78**

122

You stand and look at the three doors.

To enter the red door, go to **58**

To enter the green door, go to **93**

To enter the yellow door, go to **96**

The Magic Knight

123

You dive into the antique wardrobe that Miss Flopsbottom uses to store her spare robes and carefully close the door behind you. You hear Miss Brimstone and Heston enter the office arguing amongst themselves and worry that your heartbeat is so loud they will hear it echoing around the wardrobe. There is so much dust on the floor and in the air that you have to pinch your nose to hold in a sneeze.

You crouch down and pull a pile of robes over your head and smile as a gold coin rolls out onto the floor. **Congratulations, you've found one of the gold coins!**

You hear Miss Brimstone telling Heston off for trying to snoop around

The Magic Knight

the office and let out a loud sneeze as soon as you finally hear them leave the office and lock the door behind them.

You step out of the wardrobe and laugh as Trixie climbs out from under the headmistress's desk, Colin, having transformed into a poodle, hops down from the windowsill and Gloria, now a bat, flaps down from the ceiling.

Despite the near miss, you decide to have a quick look around the room before leaving. Go to **28**

124

Once you are all in the room, Heston strikes a match and lights the torches around the walls. In the middle of the room is a big wooden table with lots of different glass jars

The Magic Knight

on top. Each one contains a different coloured liquid; some fizzing and green, others lumpy and bright pink and one is even crystal clear and filled with tiny blue fish that are swimming around upside down.

Heston explains that he has managed to steal a recipe for a potion that will cause anybody who drinks it to freeze solid for a whole day. He laughs a crazy laugh and says he plans on mixing it into the teacher's milk so that they all drink it in their morning coffee.

He says that once they are all frozen, he plans to run around the school and steal all of the magical artifacts. Once he has them all, he is sure, he will be able to rule the world!

Go to **111**

The Magic Knight

125

You step through the door and realise that the room on the other side is not empty. Huddled around a smoking beaker of green liquid are three older witches, each one dressed in a black coat and tall, black hat.

You hear one of them start to chant, "Hubble, bubble, toil and... oh now who's this? You can't get a minute's peace in this place!"

Suddenly, one of the witches raises her wand and flicks it towards you.

Roll a dice.

If you roll even, go to **18**

If you roll an odd number, go to **40**

The Magic Knight

126

   You wake up just as the sun is breaking through the curtains and go back over your first day at Monstacademy. It was certainly more eventful than you expected!

   You head down to the common room and find Gloria, Colin and Trixie already up. Gloria is looking confused as Colin and Trixie try to get her to remember as much as she can about the old stories of the Magic Knight but she can't remember anything new, no matter how hard she tries.

   You decide that you are going to have to do some research for yourselves to find out just how powerful this suit of armour is. Students are allowed out of their rooms to visit the library if needed

The Magic Knight

but Trixie is also convinced that you need to speak to Miss Flopsbottom to find out more. It is left to you to decide where to go first.

To visit the library, go to **45**

To visit Miss Flopsbottom, go to **77**

127

You make up your mind and decide to stick with Heston and his friends for now. Heston leads the way towards the tall bell tower at the back of the school and you follow on behind Kevin, an unfortunate boy who ended up with a pumpkin for a head after a disastrous magical incident. You wander to and fro from one corridor to another until you come to the bottom of a flight of old, stone stairs. You quickly climb them until you reach a locked wooden door.

The Magic Knight

Heston tells you that to prove that you are loyal to him and that he can trust you, you must pick the door with a set of magical lock picks. He opens a roll of black felt and inside are several slim silver rods. Each one has a tip that glows in a different colour.

Roll a dice.

If you roll an even number go to **2**

If you roll an odd number go to **11**

Want to read more?

Use the code **SUPERFAN** to get **10% off*** any books at

http://mattbeighton.co.uk

* Offer may be withdrawn at any time without notice. Excludes Monstacademy complete sets. Excludes P&P charges. Offer not valid at other retailers or websites.

Also Available!

Trixie Grimble is a perfectly ordinary girl. Unfortunately, the children at her new school are not. Monstacademy is a school for monsters.

To make matters even worse, Trixie gets caught up in an evil plan to get rid of all of the ordinary people down in the village. With only a vegetarian vampire and a cursed werewolf for support, can Trixie save the day or will she be expelled forever?

Find out in The Halloween Parade.

A new term means new trouble for Trixie Grimble and the rest of the Monstacademy gang.

Can Trixie win her first Snaffleball match? Can she solve an Ancient Egyptian theft? Why is Miss Flopsbottom acting so weird?

Find out in **The Egyptian Treasure**.

To make sure you are one of the first to know all about Trixie's latest adventures, join the newsletter at http://www.mattbeighton.co.uk

About The Author

Matt Beighton is a full-time writer, born somewhere in the Midlands in England during the heady days of the 1980s. He is happily married with two young daughters who keep him very busy and suffer through the endless early drafts of his stories.

Matt's books have been read around the world and awarded the LoveReading4Kids "Indie Books We Love" and Readers' Favorite 5 Star Awards.

Having spent many years as a primary-school teacher, Matt Beighton knows how to bring stories to life. He regularly visits schools and runs creative workshops that ignite a passion for words.

If you have enjoyed reading this book, please leave a review online. Your words really do keep me going!

To find out more visit
www.mattbeighton.co.uk

Printed in Great Britain
by Amazon